Reading together is fun with
SHARE-A-STORY

SHARE-A-STORY books—
what they are and how they work:

What They Are

Many adults want to encourage children to read, but have difficulty in finding really suitable stories. SHARE-A-STORY books have been devised by Pat Thomson for just this purpose—to help adults and children enjoy reading together. Here you have fresh, entertaining stories illustrated by top artists, for adult and child to explore between them.

How They Work

First, the adult reads the whole story aloud to the child. As the child gains in confidence, the story develops as a "conversation" between the two. The right- and left-hand pages are arranged so that adult and child "take turns" as the story unfolds, with the right-hand page simpler than the left. Eventually the child will be able to read the whole story without adult support, and even share it with friends.

GOOD GIRL GRANNY

by
Pat Thomson
Illustrated by
Faith Jaques

A Young Yearling Book

Published by
Dell Publishing
a division of
The Bantam Doubleday Dell Publishing Group, Inc.
666 Fifth Avenue
New York, New York 10103

This work was first published in Great Britain by Victor Gollancz Ltd.

ISBN: 0-440-40026-0

Reprinted by arrangement with Delacorte Press

Printed in the United States of America

March 1988

10 9 8 7 6 5 4 3 2

W

GOOD GIRL
GRANNY

Help!
Granny, look what I've done.
My bread fell on the floor
and I've got yucky butter.

What a child!
Now I've got buttered carpet.
You children today are all the same.
When I was young,
we had to behave ourselves.
Mind you, it reminds me of the time
I sat in the sandwiches.

You really sat in the sandwiches?
Did you, Granny?
How did you ever do that?

I was just carrying the tray
when I lost my balance.
That's all.
I was wearing my skates.

What a mess.
You must have had a buttered bottom.
Did you ever do anything naughty?

Certainly not.
Parents were very strict then.
Mind you, there was the time
we took the cat out
dressed in the baby's clothes.

Did anyone see you?
Did the cat jump out?
It must have looked funny
in the baby's clothes.

The cat liked it.
He wore a frilly bonnet
and snoozed peacefully.
Mrs. Clark asked how Baby was.
We said, "Quite well, thank you."
We were very polite children.

Mrs. Clark must have had a shock
when she looked.
I wish I'd seen a cat with a bonnet,
sleeping like a baby.
Were you ever naughty at school?

Good gracious, no!
We didn't dare.
Mind you, there was the time
I dressed the mop
in teacher's clothes.

Granny! That's awful.
Did you really do something
so terrible?
Tell me right now.
I want to hear this.

I was very young at the time.
It was nothing really.
Teacher and I disagreed
so she made me stand in the closet.

In the closet!
I don't know anyone else
who has been put in a closet.
Was it dark?

No, no.
It was more like a little cloakroom.
Teacher's outdoor clothes were there.
I put her feathered hat on the mop,
buttoned the coat around it,
and tied on the scarf.

I wish I'd been there.
Were your friends ever naughty, too?
Tell me about the sort of things
you used to do with your friends.

We were only allowed to play
with nice children, of course.
We never had the chance
to get into real mischief.
Mind you, there was the matter
of the empty apple pie.

Granny!
Did you even manage to be naughty
with an apple pie?
How was it empty?
This is like a mystery story.

My mother gave a party, you see.
My friends and I saw the food.
The pie looked delicious.
I'm afraid we took off the pastry
and ate up the middle.
We put in some cotton instead.

You ate up all the apple
and put the lid back?
Everyone must have been cross.
Did you get into trouble?

Not as much as when we made
Cousin Edward some special medicine.
We meant well, naturally.
We thought it would cure his cold.

Imagine making it yourself, Granny.
What sort of medicine was it?
Did he spit and splutter
or was it nice?

Interesting, dear.
It tasted interesting.
It was hot water,
a nice spoonful of jam,
a piece of coal, and,
something we found under the stove.

Poor Edward. Jam is all right.
Coal might be interesting,
but what if that something
under the stove was a dead mouse?
How old was Edward when he died?

Eighty-seven, dear.
I expect the hot water did him good.
Ah yes, we had to amuse ourselves
when I was young.

You did amuse yourself, Granny.
You seem to have been naughty
in the kitchen, at school, indoors,
outdoors, everywhere.

Naughty, my dear?
I wouldn't say I was ever naughty.
We had to behave in my day.
You modern children have
much more fun.
Have some more bread and jam.